No Moon, No Milk!

Moon, No Milk!

by CHRIS BABCOCK

illustrated by MARK TEAGUE

Dragonfly Books™

Crown Publisher

When Rob came to milk his cow one early morning, he found that her udder was dry and her eyes were wet.

"Martha, you're crying. Are you sick?" Rob asked.

"Yes! Sick of being a cow! It's eat grass, get milked. Eat grass, get milked." Martha drew in a quivering breath. "I want to do more than cow around in a pasture all my life!"

"Where else *would* you like to cow around?" Rob asked as he looked into his empty bucket.

"The mooooon," Martha announced.

"You can only go to the moon if you're an astronaut," Rob said.

"Or a cowsmonaut!" Martha declared.

"I'm not sure they let cattle into the space program," Rob said.

"My great-great-grandmother jumped over the moon. If she can jump it, I can walk it."

"But I never promised you the moon!" Rob said. "Now do me a favor and let down some milk."

Martha shook her head back and forth, flinging her tears through the air. "NO MOON, NO MILK!" she bellowed.

But Rob knew there was no way to take Martha to the moon,
so he took her to Venice Beach in Southern California instead.

"Hang ten, Martha!" Rob shouted. "Did you know there's not a drop of water for surfing on the moon?"

"Cows don't surf," Martha said.

"I know, I know," Rob said. "No moon, no milk."

"NO MOOOOON, NO MILK," Martha confirmed.

But Rob knew there was no way to take Martha to the moon,
so he took her to Crater Lake National Park in Oregon instead.

"Look, Martha. A real crater," Rob said.

"I'll bet craters on the moon are much more mysterious," Martha grumbled.

"But Martha! A cow won't fit into a space capsule!" Rob cried.

"NO MOOOOON, NO MILK," she said. "I'm telling you."

But Rob knew he couldn't take Martha to the moon, so he took
her to Radio City Music Hall in New York City instead.

"Martha, it's the Rockettes!" Rob said.

"Rockets! Where are the rockets?" Martha asked, craning her neck.
"Not rockets, Martha. Rockettes! And you can bet there's no dancing like *that* on the moon!"

"I don't want to dance on the moon. I just want to walk on it!" Martha wailed. And as she took off down the aisle and out the doors, she cried, "And if you won't take me to the moon, I'll get there by myself!"

Rob threw up his hands in frustration and ran after his stampeding cow.

When he saw she was heading for Central Park, he hopped a bus,
hoping to head her off uptown.

    Meanwhile, Martha caught up to a passel of skaters darting through the park.

    "Excuse me, but could you direct me to the moon?" Martha asked as she trotted alongside them.

    "Follow this path, then hang a left at the fountain," a skater replied. Martha mooed her thanks and galloped on.

Rob had just gotten off the bus across from the American Museum of Natural History when Martha rounded the corner and came to a complete hoof-sliding halt in front of him.

"A science moooseum?" Martha moaned. "What on earth can a cow do in a science moooseum?"

"There's a replica of the lunar surface you can walk on," Rob offered.

Martha was already across the street and through the front
doors of the museum before Rob finished his sentence.

"Restrain that bovine!" a guard cried as Martha galloped by. "I hope this works," Rob said to himself as he borrowed a space helmet from a display case and ran after his cow.

Meanwhile, Martha had lost the guard in the Domesticated Animals exhibit.

"I swear I saw a cow run through here!" the guard exclaimed to the curious onlookers.

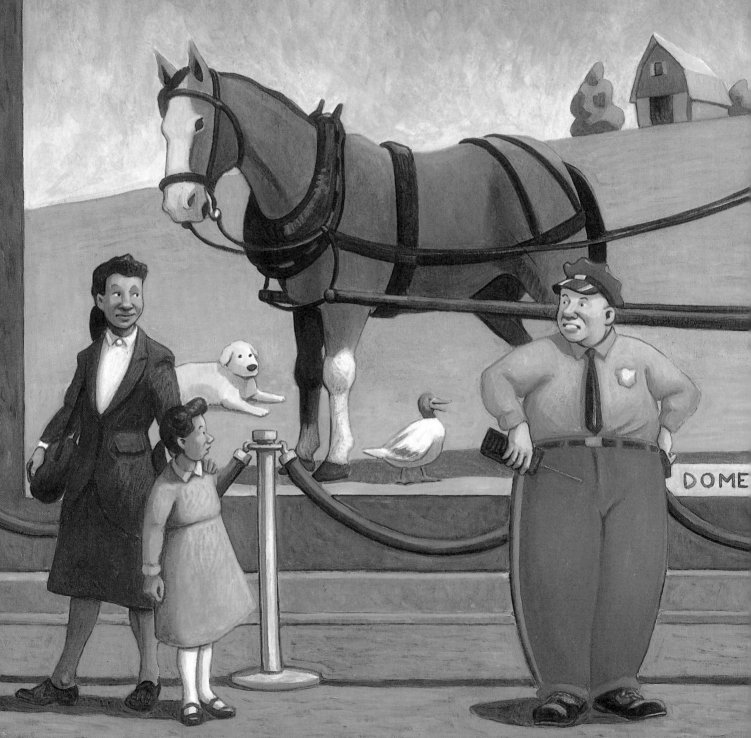

As soon as the crowd and the guard had disappeared, Martha headed for the moon. Rob was waiting for her there with the space helmet.

"I pronounce Martha Bovine a true cowsmonaut," Rob said as he slipped the helmet on her head. Then Rob unhooked the red rope that hung across the path to the lunar surface and bowed.

As Martha put her first hoof on the moon, she said, "One small step for cow, one giant leap for cowkind."

Martha had walked all the way over to where the American flag was planted when the guard finally found her. "Cow on the moon! Cow on the moon!" the guard shouted.

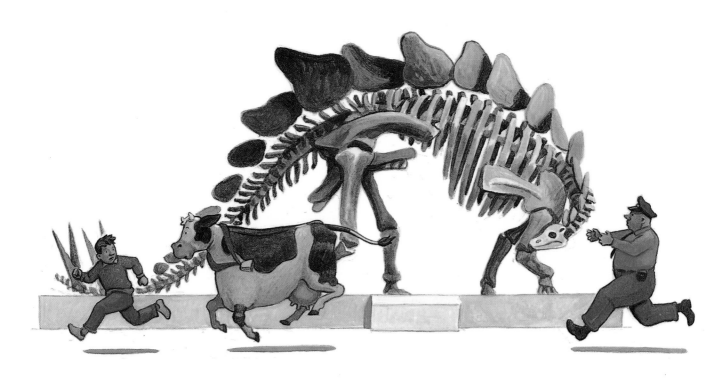

"Back to Earth, Martha!" Rob yelled, and they both ran through the museum and out the back exit, leaving the breathless guard far behind.

"So how was it to cow around on the moon, Martha?" Rob asked as he squirted milk into his bucket the very next morning.

"Oh, it was okay," Martha said.

"Okay!" Rob exclaimed. "Just okay?"

"Yeah. Now I know why my great-great-grandmother didn't stop to cow around up there."

"Why?" asked Rob.

"There's no grass," Martha said.

To Jonathan Eaton — C.B.

DRAGONFLY BOOKS™ PUBLISHED BY CROWN PUBLISHERS, INC.
Text copyright © 1993 by Chris Babcock
Illustrations copyright © 1993 by Mark Teague

Published by Crown Publishers, Inc., a Random House company,
201 East 50th Street, New York, NY 10022.
Originally published in hardcover by Crown Publishers, Inc., in 1993.
CROWN is a trademark of Crown Publishers, Inc.
Manufactured in the United States of America

Library of Congress Cataloging-in-Publication Data
Babcock, Chris.
No moon, no milk! / by Chris Babcock; illustrated by Mark Teague.
p. cm.
Summary: Martha the cow refuses to give milk until she can visit the moon like her great-great-
grandmother before her, the Cow Who Jumped Over the Moon.
[1. Cows—Fiction. 2. Moon—Fiction.] I. Teague, Mark, ill. II. Title.
PZ7.B12114No   1993
[E]—dc20   92-40697
ISBN 0-517-58779-3 (trade)
0-517-58780-7 (lib. bdg.)
0-517-88540-9 (pbk.)

10 9 8 7 6 5 4 3

First Dragonfly Books Edition: August 1995